Hey, Coaches! Thanks for your patience, dedication, and good humor. —L. A.

Dedicated to my #1 team, the Smiths. —K. S.

STERLING CHILDREN'S BOOKS
New York

An Imprint of Sterling Publishing Co., Inc.
1166 Avenue of the Americas
New York, NY 10036

STERLING CHILDREN'S BOOKS and the distinctive Sterling Children's Books
logo are trademarks of Sterling Publishing Co., Inc.

Text © 2016 by Linda Ashman
Illustrations © 2016 by Kim Smith

ISBN 978-1-4549-1607-9

Distributed in Canada by Sterling Publishing Co., Inc.
c/o Canadian Manda Group, 664 Annette Street
Toronto, Ontario, Canada M6S 2C8
Distributed in the United Kingdom by GMC Distribution Services
Castle Place, 166 High Street, Lewes, East Sussex, England BN7 1XU
Distributed in Australia by Capricorn Link (Australia) Pty. Ltd.
P.O. Box 704, Windsor, NSW 2756, Australia

For information about custom editions, special sales, and premium and
corporate purchases, please contact Sterling Special Sales at 800-805-5489
or specialsales@sterlingpublishing.com.

Manufactured in China
Lot #:
2 4 6 8 10 9 7 5 3 1
05/16

www.sterlingpublishing.com

Designed by Andrea Miller
The artwork for this book was created digitally.

Hey, Coach!

by Linda Ashman • illustrated by Kim Smith

STERLING CHILDREN'S BOOKS
New York

1ST PRACTICE

Hey, Coach!

Guess what?
I'm on your team.
Can we be blue?
No, red.
No, green!

Let's be the  TIGERS.

No, the SHARKS.

The  UNICORNS.

The BEARS.

The SPARKS!

I can dribble.
I can throw.
Watch me kick this.

THWACK!

Uh, oh.

collide.

I *think* I'm ready.
Can I play?

Oh . . . we run the *other* way?

GAME #2
1 6

Hey, Coach!

I dribbled—then I tripped.
I tried to kick it, but I slipped.
Can't use my hands?
Oops, I forgot.
This is harder than I thought.

Help! My shin guards won't stay on.
Coach—my jersey's *way* too long.
My shorts are loose.
My cleats are tight.
Did I put on my pinny right?

That was fun.
I ran a lot.
Next time, Coach,
I'll take a shot.

GAME #3

2 4

Hey, Coach—

See that? It hit the post!
I nearly scored a goal—
almost!

This week I'm going to practice more.
I really, *really* want to score.

GAME #5

3 4

That was close!
We almost tied.
We shake hands with the other side.

Who brought the snacks?

Can I have two?

There's one more left, Coach—
just for you.

It's not *that* wet.
The field's okay.
It's clearing up.
Can we still play?

I did it, Coach!
I passed the ball.

I kicked it hard.

I didn't fall.

I blocked the shot.

I dribbled fast.

Hey, Coach—

I'm sad.
Our season's done.
I *love* this game.
It's so much fun.

I'll play next year.
Can't wait till then—

Can I be on your team again?

NEVER GIVE UP
Tu
W
Th
F
Sa
1
2 GAME #5 3-4
6
7 Practice 4PM
8
9 GAME #6 CANCELED
13
14 Practice 4PM
15
16 GAME #7 7-5
20
21
22
23 PIZZA PARTY!
27
28
29
30
Practice 4PM
Practice 4PM
Simon
Anne
Jenny
THANK YOU!
Kyra
Grace
Luke
Doug
Eli
Nico
Kate